But All My Friends Smoke

CIGARETTES AND PEER PRESSURE

Tobacco: The Deadly Drug

Born to Smoke: Nicotine and Genetics

Burning Money: The Cost of Smoking

But All My Friends Smoke:
Cigarettes and Peer Pressure

But Smoking Makes Me Happy: The Link Between
Nicotine and Depression

Cash Crop to Cash Cow:
The History of Tobacco and Smoking in America

False Images, Deadly Promises:
Smoking and the Media

No More Butts: Kicking the Tobacco Habit

Putting Out the Fire: Smoking and the Law

Smokeless Tobacco: Not a Safe Alternative

Teenagers and Tobacco:
Nicotine and the Adolescent Brain

Thousands of Deadly Chemicals:
Smoking and Health

But All My Friends Smoke

CIGARETTES AND PEER PRESSURE

by
Lesli B. Evans

But All My Friends Smoke: Cigarettes and Peer Pressure

MASON CREST PUBLISHERS INC.
370 Reed Road
Broomall, Pennsylvania 19008
(866)MCP-BOOK (toll free)
www.masoncrest.com

First Printing

9 8 7 6 5 4 3 2 1

ISBN 978-1-4222-0239-5
ISBN 978-1-4222-0230-2 (series)
        Library of Congress Cataloging-in-Publication Data

Evans, Lesli
   But all my friends smoke : cigarettes and peer pressure / by
Lesli B. Evans.
      p. cm. — (Tobacco: the deadly drug)
Includes bibliographical references and index.
   ISBN 978-1-4222-0239-5   ISBN 978-1-4222-1327-8
1. Smoking—Juvenile literature. 2. Peer pressure—Juvenile lit-
erature. I. Title.
   HV5745.E94 2009
   613.85—dc22
                              2008019475

Design by MK Bassett-Harvey.
Produced by Harding House Publishing Service, Inc.
www.hardinghousepages.com
Cover design by Peter Culotta.
Printed in The United States of America.

Contents

Introduction *6*

1 Good Pressure, Bad Pressure *11*

2 How Peer Pressure Gets to People *31*

3 Why Smoke in the First Place? *49*

4 Everyone Smokes: Truth or Lie? *63*

5 Think on Your Feet *81*

6 Somebody to Help *95*

Further Reading *104*

For More Information *105*

Bibliography *107*

Index *109*

Picture Credits *111*

Author/Consultant Biographies *112*

Introduction

Tobacco has been around for centuries. In fact, it played a major role in the early history of the United States. Tobacco use has fallen into and out of popularity, sometimes based on gender roles or class, or more recently, because of its effects on health. The books in the Mason Crest series TOBACCO: THE DEADLY DRUG, provide readers with a look at many aspects of tobacco use. Most important, the series takes a serious look at why smoking is such a hard habit to break, even with all of the available information about its harmful effects.

The primary ingredient in tobacco products that keeps people coming back for another cigarette is nicotine. Nicotine is a naturally occurring chemical in the tobacco plant. As plants evolved over millions of years, they developed the ability to produce chemical defenses against being eaten by animals. Nicotine is the tobacco plant's chemical defense weapon. Just as too much nicotine can make a person feel dizzy and nauseated, so the same thing happens to animals that might otherwise eat unlimited quantities of the tobacco plant.

Nicotine, in small doses, produces mildly pleasurable (rewarding) experiences, leading many people to dose themselves repeatedly throughout the day. People carefully dose themselves with nicotine to maximize the rewarding experience. These periodic hits of tobacco also help people avoid unpleasant (toxic) effects, such as dizziness, nausea, trembling, and sweating, which can occur when someone takes in an excessive amount of nicotine. These unpleasant effects are sometimes seen when a person smokes for the first time.

Although nicotine is the rewarding component of cigarettes, it is not the cause of many diseases that trouble smokers, such as lung cancer, heart attacks, and strokes. Many of the thousands of other chemicals in the cigarette are responsible for the increased risk for these diseases among smokers. In some cases, medical research has identified cancer-causing chemicals in the burning cigarette. More research is needed, because our understanding of exactly how cigarette smoking causes many forms of cancer, lung diseases (emphysema, bronchitis), heart attacks, and strokes is limited, as is our knowledge on the effects of secondhand smoke.

The problem with smoking also involves addiction. But what is addiction? Addiction refers to a pattern of behavior, lasting months to years, in which a person engages in the intense, daily use of a pleasure-producing (rewarding) activity, such as smoking. This type of use has medically and personally negative effects for the person. As an example of negative medical consequences, consider that heavy smoking (nicotine addiction) leads to heart attacks and lung cancer. As an example of negative personal consequences, consider that heavy smoking may cause a loss of friendship, because the friend can't tolerate the smoke and/or the odor.

Nicotine addiction includes tolerance and withdrawal. New smokers typically start with fewer than five cigarettes per day. Gradually, as the body becomes adapted to the presence of nicotine, greater amounts are required to obtain the same rewarding effects, and the person eventually smokes fifteen to twenty or more cigarettes per day. This is tolerance, meaning that more drug is needed to achieve the same rewarding effects. The brain becomes "wired" differently after long-term exposure to nicotine, allowing the brain to tolerate levels of nicotine that would otherwise be toxic and cause nausea, vomiting, dizziness and anxiety.

When a heavy smoker abruptly stops smoking, irritability, headache, sleeplessness, anxiety, and difficulty concentrating all develop within half a day and trouble the smoker for one to two weeks. These withdrawal effects are generally the opposite of those produced by the drug. They are another external sign that the brain has become wired differently because of long-term exposure to nicotine. The withdrawal effects described above are accompanied by craving. For the nicotine addict, craving is a state of mind in which having a cigarette seems the most important thing in life at the moment. For the nicotine addict, craving is a powerful urge to smoke.

Nicotine addiction, then, can be understood as heavy, daily use over months to years (with tolerance and withdrawal), despite negative consequences. Now that we have definitions of *nicotine* and *addiction*, why read the books in this series? The answer is simple: tobacco is available everywhere to persons of all ages. The books in the series TOBACCO: THE DEADLY DRUG are about understanding the beginnings, natural history, and consequences of nicotine addiction. If a teenager smokes at least one cigarette daily for a month, that person has an 80 percent chance of becoming a lifetime, nicotine-addicted, daily smoker, with all the negative consequences.

But the series is not limited to those topics. What are the characteristic beginnings of nicotine addiction? Nicotine addiction typically begins between the ages of twelve and twenty, when most young people decide to try a first cigarette. Because cigarettes are available everywhere in our society, with little restriction on purchase, nearly everyone is faced with the decision to take a puff from that first cigarette. Whether this first puff leads to a lifetime of nicotine addiction depends on several factors. Perhaps the most important factor is DNA (genetics), as twin studies tell us that most of the risk for nicotine addiction is genetic, but there is a large role for nongenetic factors (environment), such as the smoking habits of friends. Research is needed to identify the specific genetic and environmental factors that shape a person's decision to continue to smoke after that first cigarette. Books in the series also address how peer pressure and biology affect one's likelihood of smoking and possibly becoming addicted.

It is difficult to underestimate the power of nicotine addiction. It causes smokers to continue to smoke despite life-threatening events. When heavy smokers have a heart attack, a life-threatening event often directly related to smoking, they spend a week or more in the hospital where they cannot smoke. So they are discharged after enforced abstinence. Even though they realize that smoking contributed strongly to the heart attack, half of them return to their former smoking habits within three weeks of leaving the hospital. This decision to return to smoking increases the risk of a second heart attack. Nicotine addiction can influence powerfully the choices we make, often prompting us to make choices that put us at risk.

TOBACCO: THE DEADLY DRUG doesn't stop with the whys and the hows of smoking and addiction. The series includes books that provide readers with tools they can use to not take that first cigarette, how they can stand up to negative peer pressure, and know when they are being unfairly influenced by the media. And if they do become smokers, books in the series provide information about how they can stop.

If nicotine addiction can be a powerful negative effect, then giving people information that might help them decide to avoid—or stop—smoking makes sense. That is what TOBACCO: THE DEADLY DRUG is all about.

— *Wade Berrettini MD, PhD*

CHAPTER

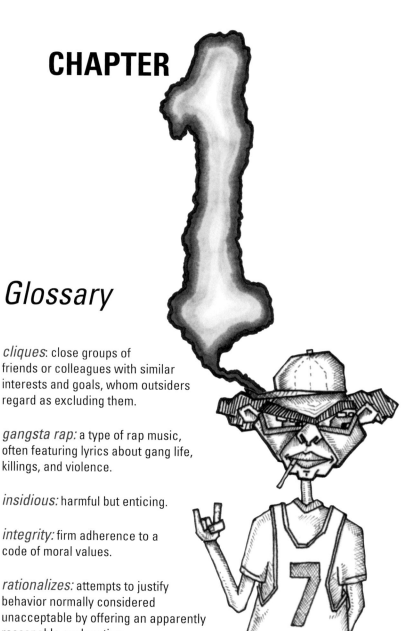

Glossary

cliques: close groups of friends or colleagues with similar interests and goals, whom outsiders regard as excluding them.

gangsta rap: a type of rap music, often featuring lyrics about gang life, killings, and violence.

insidious: harmful but enticing.

integrity: firm adherence to a code of moral values.

rationalizes: attempts to justify behavior normally considered unacceptable by offering an apparently reasonable explanation.

stereotypes: oversimplified images or ideas, often incomplete and inaccurate, held by one person or a group about another.

Good Pressure, Bad Pressure

Megan was anxious about starting high school. She was shy, and making friends had never been easy for her. Now, as if going to a new and much larger school weren't scary enough, the very best friend she ever had would be attending another school.

"Hi! Are you new? I'm Mara."

Megan turned at the strange voice. "Yes. I'm Megan."

"Well, Megan, so am I—new, that is. I can't believe how much bigger this school is than my last school."

As the two new students got acquainted, another girl joined them. "Hi. I'm Carly. Are you guys as nervous as I am?" Megan and Mara nodded in agreement. "Good. That gives us something in common," Carly said.

The girls quickly discovered that they had much more in common than the "first day at a new school" jitters. They didn't have any of the same classes, but Megan, Mara, and Carly made sure to get together whenever they could. When the first week of classes was over, the girls celebrated with a sleepover at Carly's house.

Teenagers experience pressure to "fit in" almost 24 hours a day, 7 days a week. If all her friends smoke, a teen may find it very hard to say no.

"Girls, let me know if you need anything. Otherwise, you're on your own," Carly's mother said after the girls had settled in.

"Thanks, Mom," Carly called as she shut the door to her room. The girls were sitting on the floor, eating pizza and comparing notes about their first week in high school. Carly went to her book bag, reached inside, and pulled out a pack of cigarettes and a lighter. Megan and Mara looked at each other as Carly expertly lit a cigarette and took a drag. "Hey girls, want one?"

"Uh, no," answered Mara, shaking her head.

"Megan?" Carly offered the pack to Megan.

Megan started to reach for the cigarettes. *She's smoking in the house . . . her mom must not even mind*, she thought. But just as her hand reached the pack, Mara's hand came down on her arm—hard. "Megan, what are you doing? You know it's bad to smoke. We've been told it's bad for our health all our lives. And besides, it's illegal."

"Oh, Mara. One is not going to hurt you. Besides, we're young. We have plenty of time to quit. It's just a way to relax," Carly said.

Megan looked at her new friends and asked herself, *What should I do?*

The entire human race has a built-in need for social acceptance. It's part of being human, and it gives most of us a strong urge to "fit in" with the crowd.

This human need is the key reason most people are susceptible to peer pressure—the influence that people who are like each other have on each other. Peer groups are often made up of individuals around the same age. They may be neighborhood friends, members of *cliques* at school, classmates, or coworkers. Your peers might also be teammates or belong to your religious group or even your family. Peer pressure starts early and continues through-out life.

In some ways, human beings are pack animals; like wolves, we do best when we live together in groups, rather than as loners. Our human "packs" follow certain unspoken rules, just as wolf packs do. Wherever and whenever social interactions take place, peers exert pressure on one another to conform to certain values and behaviors.

And yet as human beings, especially human beings from the Western civilization that began with the ancient Greeks and Romans, we also value our own unique individuality; we want to be true to our own selves. Learning to recognize situations in which peer pressure is exerted can strengthen your ability to make choices and decisions that reflect your own thinking and values. If you feel pressure to do or say things, or to behave in a way that makes you feel uncomfortable, you will be bet-ter prepared to make the best decision and do what is right for you.

Positive Peer Pressure

"Good" or "positive" peer pressure occurs when its influences and effects are good for you. Mara is exerting positive pressure when she reminds Megan that they've been taught that smoking is not good for them. Here's another example. Suppose most of your friends work hard at school, get good grades, and often talk about going to college. If you hang out with this group, you are likely to conform to the group's values and develop similar work habits and goals. This type of peer pressure can have a strong, positive, and long-lasting impact on you.

This same type of good peer pressure could be exerted on an adult in the workplace. An employee who surrounds herself with coworkers who like their jobs, take their work seriously, try their best to perform well, and have high ambitions in life, is likely to be positively affected by her associations with this peer group.

Negative Peer Pressure

"Bad" or "negative" peer pressure occurs when the influences and effects have undesirable consequences

The phrase "peer pressure" is immediately associated with negative activities: drinking, doing drugs, smoking. But peer pressure can be a positive force as well, to encourage your friends to "do the right thing."

for you or someone else. For example, some people do not want their children to listen to certain types of music or to particular musical artists, like those producing *gangsta rap*. Even a teenager who has never heard such music may be attracted to it if her perception is that "all the kids at school" are listening to it. She feels "left out" when her friends discuss songs by certain rappers. She longs to be part of the group and thinks that listening to this music is necessary to achieve that. Her parents,

A student whose friends exert a positive influence on him will be more likely to avoid negative individuals and situations.

on the other hand, may not believe anything positive can come from listening to lyrics they find offensive. The words and images evoked in much of this music may be completely opposed to the values of their family. They may fear that listening to gangsta rap may lead their daughter to participate in other activities that they don't approve of. They see the peer group their daughter wants to fit in with as a negative influence in her life.

In the story that opened the chapter, Carly is exerting negative peer pressure; she *rationalizes* why smoking isn't all that bad for the girls. This is a real-life situation. Suppose your closest friend starts to hang out with people who smoke cigarettes. He smokes with them, not because he likes to smoke, but because he wants to fit in with his new friends. No matter what you say, your friend smokes even though he never would have before, just to fit in with the group. It's clear to you that your friend lacks the self-confidence to resist the social pressure of his new friends. He has conformed to their values instead of honoring his own. Even the most well-informed and intelligent people can make poor choices because of negative peer pressure. In the case of smoking, the consequences of choosing to smoke can be nicotine addiction and major health problems.

Sometimes negative peer pressure is obvious. It is direct—right out in the open—and it is clear that someone wants you to do something that is not good for you or for someone else. Though much of the talk about the effects of negative peer pressure centers on teens, people of all ages can be influenced by negative peer pressure. They may be susceptible to negative peer pressure because of fear or because they have not yet developed the confidence and other psychological tools that could help them resist. As you read Nick's story, see if you can identify the direct peer pressure exerted on him to smoke cigarettes.

Don't Be a Wimp, Nick

Fourteen-year-old Nick is a two-sport athlete at his school, located in the middle of North Carolina. Many of his friends and their parents work in the tobacco fields around his town. Just about everyone he knows smokes, except his football teammates. One day their coach brought in a speaker, a friend from his college football days. Beginning in high school and continuing throughout college, both the coach and his friend had been smokers. Shortly after college, Nick's coach had struggled through the quitting process successfully. His friend had tried to quit more than once, but kept falling back into the cigarette habit—that is, until he got a dire diagnosis. The former college football player was dying. Years of smoking had irreparably damaged his lungs. After hearing the speaker, Nick and his teammates promised each other they would never smoke.

One day, weeks later, Nick and some of his teammates were hanging out in a park at the edge of town. There were kids from another team there, so they had enough people for a scrimmage. They all had a great time playing football. When they flopped onto the grass to rest after the game, Nick sat next to Gary, a tall defensive tackle from the other team. Nick told Gary, "Good game! We could use your speed on our defense."

Gary responded, "Yeah, thanks man. Boy, do I need a smoke! Want one?" Gary offered Nick a cigarette from his freshly opened pack.

"Naw, man. Thanks, but I don't smoke." Nick was surprised to see a guy like Gary putting a cigarette to his lips.

Gary considered Nick's statement for a second, then rolled his eyes. "C'mon man, don't be such a wimp. One cigarette won't kill you! Haven't you ever tried one? How old are you? Hey, I love football, and I can see you do too. But having a smoke after a game makes it even better. At least give it a try. It's just one."

Nick felt a shock run up his spine and looked away for a second. *Gary has blazing speed. I thought smoking messed up your lungs. It sure doesn't look like Gary has any problems breathing. I only wish I had Gary's speed.* "Why not? Sure, I'll give it a try." Nick replied so quickly it even surprised himself.

"Thanks, man," Nick remembered saying as he lit and inhaled his first cigarette. Soon he was exhaling in concert with Gary. As he exhaled, Nick thought about the health risks associated with cigarettes. He remembered the coach's friend who had talked to the team. He thought about his teammates and their promise to never smoke. Nick was a smart guy, and he understood that peer pressure was the reason he was sitting here smoking with Gary right now. Nick admired Gary's ability, and he wanted Gary's respect. He thought that to get it he had to smoke. Even though Nick had promised his team-

If all your friends are smoking, it can seem lonely to be the only person who is not. This is why even the smartest teens sometimes give in to peer pressure.

mates that he would never smoke, and he was well aware of the health risks of smoking, he could not resist Gary's influence. Nick was a strong, confident athlete, but his desire to gain Gary's respect was even stronger. Nick fell prey to his need for social approval.

Direct Peer Pressure

This type of direct peer pressure can happen whether you are young or old. For example, a man in his forties might be influenced to try chewing tobacco for the first time while on a fishing trip with friends who engage in this activity.

Direct peer pressure can be either negative or positive. Take note of how and when others say things designed to influence you. Ask yourself if the thing(s) they are suggesting will affect your life in a positive or a negative way.

The peer pressure exerted on Nick by Gary was direct, and it was negative. On the other hand, the story that opened this chapter contained an example of direct but positive peer pressure when Mara tried to talk Megan out of smoking.

Indirect Peer Pressure

Sometimes peer pressure is not as obvious as it was in the cases of Megan and Nick. A specific individual might not even be targeted. Peer pres-

Not all Peer Pressure Is Negative
Positive peer pressure encourages many of us to do things that improve our lives. We are as susceptible to positive peer pressure as we are to negative peer pressure.

sure can be indirect or unspoken. As with direct peer pressure, people of all ages can be affected by indirect peer pressure. Adults may feel pressured to buy expensive cars, houses, or other things they can't really afford just to "fit in" with wealthier friends, relatives, or other peers. This is an example of negative indirect peer pressure.

On the other hand, if an adult admires what others have, he might use that indirect peer pressure as motivation to work hard to acquire those things. If he is able to purchase the admired things later, after he can afford them (rather than going into debt because of envy, as in the previous example), the indirect peer pressure is positive.

Indirect peer pressure isn't limited to just acquiring things. If a person admires the good works someone else does, she might be influenced to participate in the same good works projects, or be moved to choose projects that are important to her.

Teenagers are not the only victims of peer pressure; adults also fall victim to influences of society. Adults fulfill the need to appear wealthy by owning expensive cars, houses, electronics or other high-status items.

For younger people, indirect peer pressure might have to do with the desire to be like someone they admire. A young person may want to dress or act like an older friend, or listen to the same music his friend likes. Read Gabbi's story below. As you read, identify the indirect peer pressure she feels to smoke cigarettes.

Gabbi's First Cigarette

Gabbi was just ten years old the first time she smoked. It happened on a Friday. It must have been a Friday, because Gabbi remembered that she had been excited all day, the way she was only on Fridays. That was the day when she got to spend time alone with Kitty, her older sister. Monday through Thursday Kitty had after-school activities, and she spent all weekend with her friends. But Friday was her time with Gabbi.

To pass the hours at school as she anticipated the time when she would have Kitty's full attention,

Young kids look up to their older siblings as role models. When a big sister makes healthy choices, there is a good chance her little sister will as well.

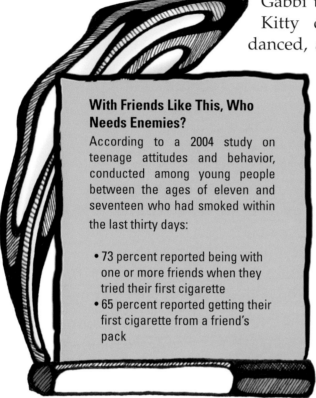

With Friends Like This, Who Needs Enemies?

According to a 2004 study on teenage attitudes and behavior, conducted among young people between the ages of eleven and seventeen who had smoked within the last thirty days:

- 73 percent reported being with one or more friends when they tried their first cigarette
- 65 percent reported getting their first cigarette from a friend's pack

Gabbi thought about how Kitty dressed, how she danced, and how she blew smoke rings from her cigarette and let them slide onto her ring finger. The smoke rings enthralled Gabbi, and she thought Kitty looked independent and glamorous holding the silver-tipped, streamlined cigarette in her tanned hand.

The long-awaited hour finally arrived, and it was time for Gabbi to head home. She bolted onto the school bus and fidgeted in her seat until it reached the bus stop where Kitty was waiting impatiently.

Gabbi noticed how great her teenage sister looked in a new pair of jeans and boots. She loved Kitty and wanted to be just like her. Gabbi remembered that day like it was yesterday. Gabbi could almost hear the desperation in Kitty's voice when she said, "Boy, do I need a smoke!"

As the sisters turned and walked toward home, Gabbi practically ran to keep up with Kitty. As soon as they rounded the corner and were far enough from the bus stop (and the eyes of the bus driver),

Kitty grabbed a lighter from her jeans pocket and lit a cigarette. She took a deep drag from her cigarette and then exhaled with a long, satisfied sigh.

Gabbi remembered wanting to be just like Kitty. She remembered the conversation that preceded her first smoke. "Let me bum a cigarette from you, Kitty," she had said, trying to sound cool.

"No, Gabbi, you're too young," Kitty had answered, slipping her arm around her little sister.

"I am not. I'm in fifth grade! I'll be in middle school next year. Please, Kitty." Gabbi remembered shouting and almost begging as she felt her face grow red at the insult.

"Okay," Kitty said as she relented. "But just one!"

"Thank you, Kitty." Gabbi felt both gratitude and excitement as she considered how lucky she was to have such a great older sister.

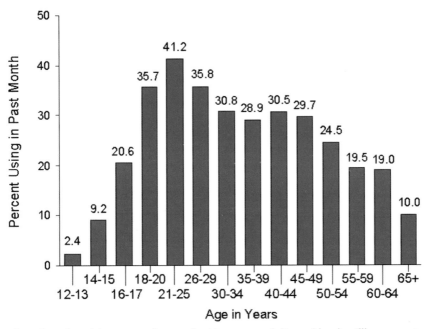

Despite advertising campaign against it, young adult smoking is still a current trend. This graph indicates that individuals in the 18-29 age group are the most likely to smoke.

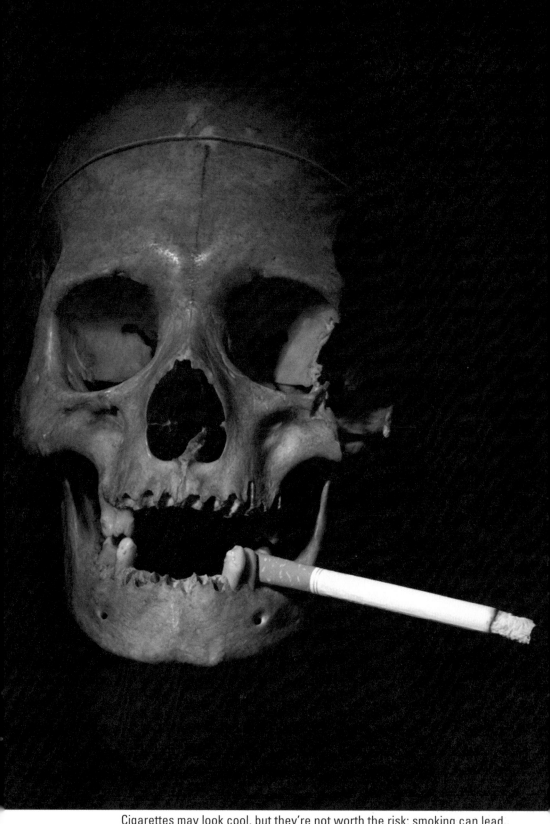

Cigarettes may look cool, but they're not worth the risk; smoking can lead to many negative health effects, including cardiovascular disease, cancer, respiratory disease, and death.

On the day Gabbi had her first cigarette, she had no idea that social pressure was the reason she had wanted to smoke. This form of indirect peer pressure is not always easy to recognize. Gabbi didn't know was what was influencing her; from Gabbi's point of view, she just wanted to be like her sister.

People are multidimensional. They can have both positive and negative characteristics at the same time. Take care to notice both the good and bad characteristics of people you admire. Understanding that each individual can exert both positive and negative influences on someone can help you resist negative peer pressure, whether it is direct or indirect.

All the stories in this chapter illustrate the human need for social acceptance, and the various forms peer pressure can take. Peer pressure can be a positive or a negative influence. It is not enough simply to understand certain key ideas about peer pressure. It is also important to connect that understanding to the ways peer pressure can shape your personality and character by influencing your thoughts, ideas, and goals.

Peer pressure may be *insidious* if those exerting the pressure make you afraid to deviate from common *stereotypes*. This type of social pressure can undermine personal strength and can make a person less well-balanced mentally and physically. The impact of negative peer pressure is profound since it may result in self-limiting behaviors or risky decision-making. In the case of choosing to smoke because of direct or indirect peer pressure, the long-term results of the decision may be life-threatening.

Smoking's Consequences

The consequences of smoking include the likelihood of nicotine addiction and major health problems. Each year approximately 438,000 people in the United States die prematurely from smoking or from exposure to second-hand smoke, the tobacco smoke unintentionally inhaled by people who do not smoke. Another 8.6 million people in the United States suffer from a serious smoking-related illness. According to health statistics, for every person who dies as a result of smoking, twenty more develop one or more serious illnesses related to tobacco use. Yet even though most people are aware of these risks, approximately 45.1 million adults in the United States are smokers.

Between 1964 and 2008, the U.S. Surgeon General—the cabinet-level chief public health officer of the United States—has issued twenty-nine reports on smoking and health. All of them have concluded that tobacco use is the single most avoidable cause of disease, disability, and death in the United States. Over the past forty years, smoking has caused almost 12 million deaths. That includes 5.5 million deaths from various forms of cardiovascular disease, 4.1 million from cancer, 2.1 million from respiratory diseases, and 94,000 infant deaths attributed to the fact that their mothers smoked during pregnancy.

These facts are useful to know. Keep them in mind as an incentive not to smoke. Think of them if you are tempted to use cigarettes or chewing tobacco. Counter peer pressure and the need for social acceptance by developing self-confidence and making the decisions that are best for your life and your long-term health.

Learning what makes people susceptible to peer pressure can motivate you to seek further information about how to develop strong, positive, personal qualities that can counterbalance negative peer pressure. Developing these qualities can help you avoid making decisions because of peer pressure that may be detrimental to you in the future.

The factors you will learn about in the next chapter are not new or fancy. You may already possess some qualities such as self-confidence and high self-esteem. Identifying factors critical to developing and maintaining *integrity* is valuable even if you are not currently struggling against negative peer pressure. Sometimes an individual's beliefs and values may change according to alterations occurring in his environment or other circumstances beyond his control. Naming and defining factors that are essential to successfully resisting peer pressure will help you hold firmly to your values. It will also make it easier for you to recognize when you need help to make the best decision in a given situation. Self-awareness is essential to being able to resist seemingly harmless or even blatantly negative peer pressure.

CHAPTER

Glossary

autonomy: personal independence and the ability to make and act on moral decisions.

emulate: to model oneself after someone else.

integral: being an essential part of something.

pulmonary: relating to the lungs.

How Peer Pressure Gets to People

Carly (Mara and Megan's friend), Gary (the football player), and Kitty (Gabbi's older sister) are all smokers. We do not know how or why they decided to start smoking. But we do know what attracted Nick and Gabbi (and probably Carly) to smoke that first cigarette. Different forms of peer pressure affected their decisions to try smoking. They were in different situations, yet they had something in common: they faced peer pressure from people they admired. While Kitty didn't offer Gabbi a cigarette directly, her smoking habit influenced Gabbi's view of smoking. Because Gabbi admired her older sister who smoked, smoking looked acceptable, even "cool," to her. Smoking seemed like a grown-up thing to do. Nick's decision to try a cigarette was in direct opposition to his earlier promise to one of his strongest peer groups (his teammates) never to smoke. But his admiration for Gary influenced him to abandon his earlier commitment, even though he had viewed smoking as an undesirable thing to do. Both Nick's and Gabbi's experiences illustrate ways peer pressure can "get to" people.

Self-Esteem and Self-Confidence

Self-esteem: pride in oneself, self-respect

Self-confidence: belief in oneself or in one's own abilities

Speaking in general terms, self-esteem is how you think and feel about yourself. People with healthy or high self-esteem usually think of themselves as competent and worthy of happiness. Low self-esteem is the opposite. People with low self-esteem lack confidence. They usually worry more about what other people think of them. Having low self-esteem can make a person more susceptible to peer pressure.

Where does self-esteem come from? How do we develop our beliefs about ourselves? Self-esteem arises out of life's successes and failures—the small ones and the big ones. It also derives from how parents and others in our lives think of us and treat us. Whether a baby is lovingly nurtured or physically abused, whether a child learns to read easily or struggles with a learning disability, whether a person is born into a wealthy family or a poor one, whether a child's father is a hardworking mechanic or a prisoner convicted of theft can all affect a person's self-esteem.

Teens may feel pressure to try smoking because of a desire to fit in, especially if they normally feel left out or alone.

Low self-esteem can lead teens to be unsure of themselves or their beliefs, making them more apt to respond to peer pressure.

Self-esteem is not static; it doesn't stay the same throughout our life. Self-esteem increases and decreases as we grow and change and encounter many experiences.

Low Self-Esteem

Low self-esteem can play a major role in a person's susceptibility to peer pressure. Although low self-esteem may be expressed differently from one individual to another, there are certain characteristics shared by most people with low self-esteem. People with low self-esteem may be intolerant of the ideas of others or disrespectful to other people. They rarely accept responsibility for their actions or take pride in their accomplishments. They may not feel worthy of any success. Low self-esteem can rob a person of the self-confidence needed to aim for challenging goals, try new activities, or accept constructive criticism. Worst of all, a person with low self-esteem may not be able to love anyone (even himself) or to accept love from another. People with low self-esteem usually don't feel competent or capable of taking control of their own lives.

How's Your Self-Esteem?

If the following describes you, your self-esteem is in good shape:

- You enjoy trying new things.
- You are comfortable in social settings.
- You enjoy working on group and individual projects.
- You know and accept your weaknesses and your strengths.
- You have an optimistic approach to life.
- When faced with a challenge, you work toward solving it rather than dwelling on the problem.

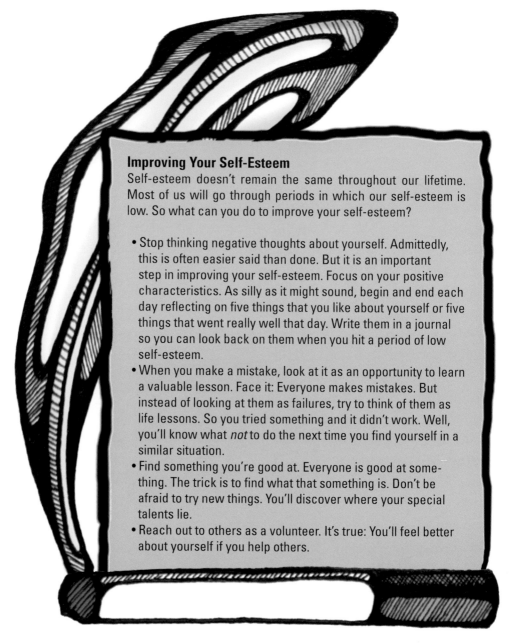

Improving Your Self-Esteem

Self-esteem doesn't remain the same throughout our lifetime. Most of us will go through periods in which our self-esteem is low. So what can you do to improve your self-esteem?

- Stop thinking negative thoughts about yourself. Admittedly, this is often easier said than done. But it is an important step in improving your self-esteem. Focus on your positive characteristics. As silly as it might sound, begin and end each day reflecting on five things that you like about yourself or five things that went really well that day. Write them in a journal so you can look back on them when you hit a period of low self-esteem.
- When you make a mistake, look at it as an opportunity to learn a valuable lesson. Face it: Everyone makes mistakes. But instead of looking at them as failures, try to think of them as life lessons. So you tried something and it didn't work. Well, you'll know what *not* to do the next time you find yourself in a similar situation.
- Find something you're good at. Everyone is good at something. The trick is to find what that something is. Don't be afraid to try new things. You'll discover where your special talents lie.
- Reach out to others as a volunteer. It's true: You'll feel better about yourself if you help others.

A period of low self-esteem doesn't mean that a person is "doomed" to never feel better about herself. Each of us has the ability to improve our attitudes, our outlook on life, and our self-esteem. There are many books and resources available with suggestions on ways to improve or boost self-esteem and self-confidence. For recommendations, check out the "Further Reading" list at the back of this book. Counseling is another option many people find helpful.

Learning to recognize factors that can make you susceptible to peer pressure is important. Do you sometimes find yourself seeking the approval and acceptance of others? Do you hide your true feelings or try to appear different than you are because you fear rejection or ridicule? Do you often feel uncertain about what you want? These are all clues that you may be susceptible to peer pressure.

Know Your Role

Uncertainty about where you fit within a peer group can increase your vulnerability to peer pressure. Wanting to be liked or being afraid of rejection may make you more susceptible to peer pressure. It might cause you to do things that conflict with your values. There may be times when you are unsure of yourself, when you don't know what you really want, or you don't know how to get out of a situation that makes you uncomfortable.

Remember Nick from chapter 1? Nick was sure he would never smoke; he and his teammates even promised each other never to smoke. But then Nick met Gary, an athlete he admired, who offered him a cigarette and then pressured him to try it. There was likely more than one reason Nick gave in to this peer pressure. He might have been afraid of rejection. Maybe he wanted to appear grown-up, or thought he'd look cool smoking. Perhaps he decided to smoke just to avoid being ridiculed. He wasn't sure how his relationship with Gary would develop, and this could have played a role in Nick's decision to smoke as well.

Maintain Personal Interests

Having no personal interests outside those of your peer group is another factor that can weaken your resistance to peer pressure. It helps to hang out with different groups at different times. If you are an athlete, you might eat and train with your teammates and go to movies or concerts with other friends or family members.

Allow time for interests of your own, whether your peer group approves of them or not. This is critical to your self-esteem. If you belong to a peer group with rigid values, and the group exerts pressure on you to conform to the point that you do not have any interests that do not include members of that group, then you become very susceptible to peer pressure.

Mary Angel's Story

This story is about Mary Angel, who moved from one state to another, changing schools and peer groups in one fell swoop. Mary Angel is an accomplished pianist and is proud of her role in the jazz band. Her new school lacks a jazz band, so she may not easily find a peer group that shares her interest and enthusiasm for jazz. If she is lucky, she will find people who share her interest in music, but if not, she will need to set aside time to enjoy jazz on her own.

Being passionate about something outside of your group of friends, like sports or music, can raise your self-esteem and make you less likely to feel you have to conform to all your friends' beliefs and values.

Mary Angel was thirteen when she and her family moved away from everything she knew and loved. It happened during the summer break before eighth grade. Mary Angel remembered that she had been practicing piano when her parents called the family together. That's when they announced that her father had received a promotion, and they would have to move before the new school year began.

Mary Angel tearfully told her friends in jazz band about her family's relocation plans and that she would not be there for their final year of middle school. Later that summer, she and her family loaded the last of their possessions into the car

Knowing that you have a skill, like Mary Angel and her jazz piano, can help you maintain a sense of self-worth even in the face of negative peer pressure.

and pulled away from the only home she had ever known.

Mary Angel and her family settled into their new house and set about the task of turning it into "home." As the summer waned, Mary began anticipating her first day of school with a mix of excitement and apprehension.

When the day finally arrived, she was a little overwhelmed as she took in all the new and different aspects of her new school and classmates. As the day wore on, she learned that the jazz band at this school had disbanded a few years earlier. *Great, now what am I supposed to do?* Mary Angel wondered. Music, jazz in particular, had been a big part of her life for longer than she could remember. Mary Angel decided that she would continue learning jazz pieces on her own while trying to find friends who might just catch the "jazz fever" she had. *I know it won't happen overnight, but maybe I'll find a jazz fan around here eventually. If not, I'll make time to feed my passion for jazz in another way. After all, it is a big part of who I am.*

So what does Mary Angel's story have to do with falling under the influence of negative peer pressure? Mary Angel has a strong sense of her self. She knows what her interests and talents are. She knows what's important to her, and she has a plan for dealing with a disappointing situation in her new school. This self-confidence can help her overcome negative peer pressure.

You've Got to Have Friends

Feeling isolated from people, or having weak ties to your peer group or family, can increase your susceptibility to all types of peer pressure. Some teens confuse freedom with *autonomy*, and this can lead them to rebel against the values held by their family or peers. This can cause difficulty or conflicts in their close relationships and weaken their social-support networks. Unfortunately, the social alienation and isolation that can result may weaken a person's ability to resist negative peer pressure.

Knowing how and where you fit into a social group can help you recognize and resist negative peer pressure.

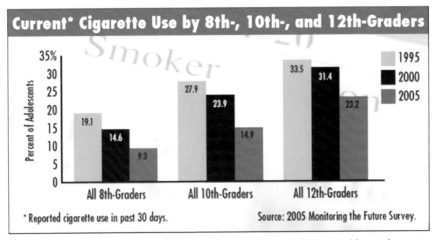

Most smokers start the habit in their teenage years. But the word is getting out, and fewer teenagers are smoking.

The Lesson So Far

You have learned how to tell when someone may be vulnerable to negative peer pressure and read about some of the key factors that can make a person particularly susceptible to it. You've acquired an understanding of the many ways peer pressure can shape an individual's personality and character, of which self-confidence and self-esteem are *integral* parts.

Fundamental to these factors is your perception of where you fit in social groups and the health of your most important relationships: those with family members and closest friends. These relationships can strongly influence your level of confidence in social situations and your ability to resist negative peer pressure. Someone who feels rejected by her family or peer group may be at risk for acting in less than positive ways just to fit in with a group—any group. When a person feels isolated, negative peer pressure can impair her ability to make decisions that reflect her own positive values. This is problematic not only because she is not being true to herself, but also because, in this situation, negative peer pressure can lure her into dangerous activities, such as smoking. To be successful in resisting peer pressure to smoke, it is necessary to clarify your ideas about where you fit in your social circles and identify the characteristics of your personality that can make you vulnerable to negative influences.

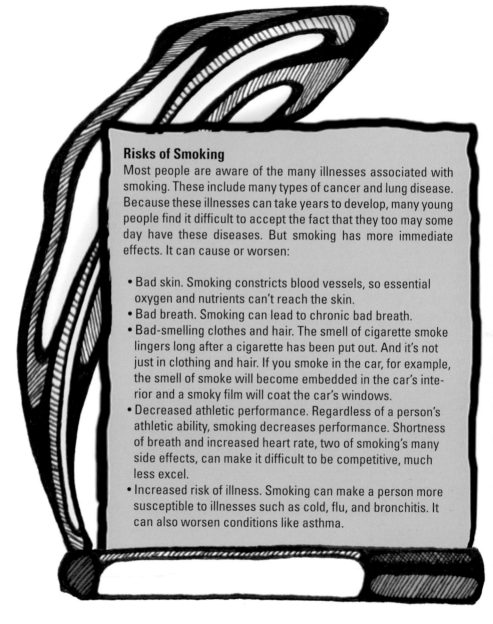

Risks of Smoking

Most people are aware of the many illnesses associated with smoking. These include many types of cancer and lung disease. Because these illnesses can take years to develop, many young people find it difficult to accept the fact that they too may some day have these diseases. But smoking has more immediate effects. It can cause or worsen:

- Bad skin. Smoking constricts blood vessels, so essential oxygen and nutrients can't reach the skin.
- Bad breath. Smoking can lead to chronic bad breath.
- Bad-smelling clothes and hair. The smell of cigarette smoke lingers long after a cigarette has been put out. And it's not just in clothing and hair. If you smoke in the car, for example, the smell of smoke will become embedded in the car's interior and a smoky film will coat the car's windows.
- Decreased athletic performance. Regardless of a person's athletic ability, smoking decreases performance. Shortness of breath and increased heart rate, two of smoking's many side effects, can make it difficult to be competitive, much less excel.
- Increased risk of illness. Smoking can make a person more susceptible to illnesses such as cold, flu, and bronchitis. It can also worsen conditions like asthma.

Other Factors

What else would make a person susceptible to negative peer pressure? Lacking goals or a direction in life, undiagnosed depression, and poor academic performance may all undermine self-esteem and make a person vulnerable to negative influences. Resources for further reading about this topic are located at the back of this book.

Critically evaluating the behavior and attitudes of people around you, as well as those of the characters in television programs or movies, is crucial if you are to maintain an awareness of direct and indirect messages

Depression can make a person more vulnerable to feelings of low self-esteem and more likely to respond to peer pressure.

about smoking. It does not matter whether these messages are overt or subtle, they may influence your attitudes about cigarettes.

What About the Media?

Though the media is not a peer, it exerts a major influence on us. Examining role models and media messages about smoking with a critical eye can help one avoid making decisions about tobacco based on faulty concepts about what it means to be "cool," "desirable," "independent," or "free." People presented in the media as role models may have qualities that you want to

There are many stereotypes about cigarettes and smoking that are spread through the media.

emulate, such as athleticism, financial success, or popularity. However, critical analysis may reveal that these positive images in the media actually mask a lie. Actors, for example, may exhibit qualities you admire—and also puff on a cigarette onscreen. This gives viewers the false impression that smoking is okay. Don't believe it. People with debilitating cardiovascular or *pulmonary* disease linked to smoking are never seen strutting their stuff in cigarette commercials, or in real life. Ads use indirect messages to "sell" smoking as being socially acceptable, even something good, without bothering to clue you in about its downside. Your peers may also do this. These half-truths wrapped in appealing social messages may influence your attitudes. Everyone needs to be aware that these messages are designed to create a feeling of inclusion—a feeling that you're *in*—among smokers.

So how can you identify such distorted messages? Get educated. Learn to recognize a media message that contains incomplete information, whether it is spoken or unspoken. Evaluate direct and indirect messages delivered by the media. Realize that the behavior of family and peers also has a strong influence on your attitudes and behaviors. You will then be prepared to evaluate situations and attitudes with a critical eye. This is essential to resisting negative influences, including those promoting smoking.

In the next chapter, you will learn various reasons people start smoking, even though they know and understand the dangers and health problems associated with cigarettes. This knowledge may help you objectively evaluate messages and attitudes about smoking delivered by family members, peers, and the media.

CHAPTER

Glossary

conformity: behaving or thinking in a socially acceptable way.

metabolic rate: the time it takes chemical interactions to occur within a living organism; these chemical reactions provide the energy and nutrients required to sustain life.

shackled: bound in chains—literally or figuratively

Why Smoke in the First Place?

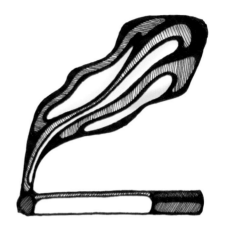

Cigarette smoking is the most preventable cause of premature death in the United States. It accounts for about 440,000 deaths each year; more than 135,000 of those deaths are due to smoking-related cardiovascular diseases. In fact, according to the American Heart Association, cigarette smokers are two to three times more likely than nonsmokers to die from coronary heart disease. Information about the negative consequences of tobacco use is everywhere. Yet, even though the health consequences are well known, thousands of people become new smokers each year. What prompts intelligent people to begin using cigarettes and to continue the habit?

Role Models

When most people take a puff from their first cigarette, they're not alone. According to a study reported in 2001 in the journal *Archives of Pediatrics & Adolescent Medicine*, only 11 percent of teens first try smoking alone.

The decision to smoke is based on a mix of social, personality, and attitudinal factors. Some kids try cigarettes simply because they are curious, while others have

Many people start smoking because someone they look up to, like a parent or guardian, smokes around them.

friends who pressure them into using tobacco. Chapter 1 discussed the built-in human need for social acceptance; in simple terms, the need to feel that we belong. This helps to explain why the habits and attitudes of their parents, siblings, and peers influence young people's attitudes and decisions about smoking. While some people think that smoking is all about freedom and independence, sometimes it is simply a sign of *conformity*.

The Role of Parents

Research studies have produced mixed results about how the smoking habits of parents affect their children. Some researchers believe that the best predictor of smoking in young people is having family members who smoke. Others believe that parental smoking does not necessarily influence the decisions of children to smoke. However, if your family members smoke, you may want to smoke to fit in. Besides, it's what you know, part of what you experienced as a child. Other times strict parental opposition to smoking can prompt young people to start smoking as a form of rebellion against parental authority. The upshot is, there may be some role models in your life who smoke and some who don't. Exactly how much influence role models have depends on you. The choice of whether you will allow the smoking habits of others to influence your decisions is up to you.

Emulating Others

Some young people start smoking because they see older people smoking and want to emulate them. They think using cigarettes makes them look more mature. Others believe smoking gives them a cool, sexy, or independent aura. Smoking by people associated with glamour, sophistication, or rebellion can also influence young people to smoke because they want to be like those people. These are all forms of indirect social pressure. In these cases, smoking can give the young person a feeling of belonging to a group of nonconforming trendsetters, those older, seemingly cool, sexy, independent, glamorous, sophisticated, or rebellious cigarette smokers. A young person's impressions about those people can influence her attitudes about smoking.

Smoke and Mirrors

Some people report that smoking helps them relax and makes it easier for them to manage stress. There is evidence that nicotine may lower anxiety and elevate mood, but its effect is short-lived. Tobacco marketers often play up these temporary positive effects to sell cigarettes, but fail to mention the downsides of smoking. The cleverly worded sales pitch does not address the health risks of a smoking habit. We are left with the task of sorting out the facts in incomplete messages, filled with half-truths, deliberate distortions, or outright lies. All of us must be aware of these kinds of indirect pressures that influence our attitudes about smoking.

Portrayals of tobacco use and references to smoking in media such as music videos, television shows, and movies convey mixed

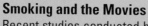

Smoking and the Movies
Recent studies conducted by Dartmouth Medical School found that the more smoking children viewed in movies, the more likely they were to try smoking. The studies were published in 2007 and 2008 in the journal Pediatrics.

The popular portrayal of smoking in the movies may make cigarettes seem more appealing, especially to young teens.

messages about smoking. Visuals may imply endorsement of smoking even when characters' words send the opposite message. Still, viewing programs or movies with indirect and direct messages about smoking can definitely influence our attitudes about smoking.

Independent or Shackled?

Tobacco companies cannot sell or market their products directly to teenagers. However, they do analyze youth markets and develop legal methods to appeal to young people who will be able to purchase their products as soon as they turn eighteen. One method used to appeal to young people is product placement. For example, a tobacco company might convince a movie company to use its brand of cigarettes or other tobacco products in a film in order to associate that brand with the celebrities in that movie. If actors and actresses in compelling stories are shown smoking as those tales unfold, people may get the impression that smoking is cool, or further, that it is linked with the qualities associated with admirable characters, such as independence, self-reliance, or courage. But the truth is that smoking isn't cool,

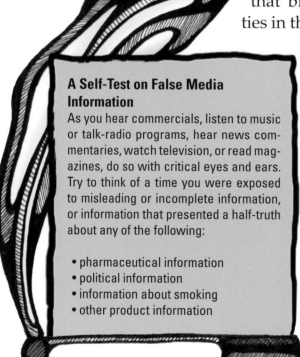

A Self-Test on False Media Information

As you hear commercials, listen to music or talk-radio programs, hear news commentaries, watch television, or read magazines, do so with critical eyes and ears. Try to think of a time you were exposed to misleading or incomplete information, or information that presented a half-truth about any of the following:

- pharmaceutical information
- political information
- information about smoking
- other product information

Cigarette companies sometimes sponsor sporting events as a way to advertise
their products. Trying to make cigarettes seem cool and exciting, these ads
leave out the harmful effects of smoking.

and it has nothing to do with independence, self-reliance, or courage. Smoking is a habit that is difficult to kick. It is more like being *shackled* than free.

Cigarette manufacturers also sponsor athletic events or other activities, where ads for their products appear prominently. These ads generally feature beautiful, healthy young people having fun. Tobacco companies create ads and promotions that link smoking with hip, sexy, slim people, but omit negative aspects such as exposure to nicotine, the substance in cigarettes that makes them highly addictive. Smokers who try to quit sometimes feel as if they were prisoners chained to their cigarette habit.

Weight Control

Some smokers believe that smoking helps them control their weight. During periods of boredom, a time when many people tend to overeat, they may smoke rather than eat. People who use cigarettes for this reason are often afraid to quit smoking because they think they'll gain weight. There is evidence that smoking does slightly raise the body's metabolic rate, so smokers may burn slightly more calories than nonsmokers. But there are much healthier ways to burn extra calories. Exercise raises the body's metabolic rate without the dangerous side effects of smoking.

Elliot's Weight Problem

Elliot was ten years old the first time he smoked. It happened because of football. Elliot had been looking forward to Pop Warner sign-ups all week. What he hadn't anticipated was having to lose fifteen pounds to play. In Pop Warner football, there are weight limits specified for each level. Elliot and

Some people believe that smoking cigarettes helps keep their weight down; however, there are much healthier ways to keep thin.

his friends Ed and Ricky all had to lose weight that year. They had been doing extra running, and they watched what they ate, but they were all having growth spurts and felt hungry all the time. Elliot often thought about how hungry he was, how cheeseburgers tasted, and how he would scarf down his food after the inevitable weigh-ins that came after each football practice. Yet, Elliot was determined to lose the weight.

Finally, it was time for Elliot to find out how many pounds he needed to lose to make the weight limit and be able to play in the first game of the season. He hopped onto the scale after practice and fidgeted until his coach looked at him and said gruffly, "Six more buddy. Think ya can lose six pounds this week, pal?"

After learning he needed to lose six more pounds, Elliot and his two friends took off and ran for several minutes, as they always did after weigh-ins. After finishing their run, they slowly walked back toward the empty field. As they walked, Ed and Ricky told Elliot that weight wouldn't be a problem for them anymore. They had a new "secret weapon" to ward off hunger. As soon as they told him, Ed grabbed a lighter from his pocket and lit a cigarette. He inhaled deeply and then exhaled with a long sigh.

As his stomach growled, Elliot longed

to make football weight, and to make his hunger go away. "Let me have one Ed," he said, trying not to sound too desperate.

"I'll take one too," Ricky chimed in.

"I'm going to quit as soon as I make weight," Elliot promised himself and his friends.

"Sure, Elliot," Ricky said skeptically.

"Watch me!" Elliot responded as he wondered how hard it would be to hide his smoking from his mom.

As he walked home that day, Elliot had no idea that social pressure was the reason he had decided to smoke. To Elliot, smoking was a tool he could use to help accomplish a positive goal: weight loss for football. And he thought, or *hoped*, he would be able to quit whenever he wanted. But it was indirect peer pressure, distorted by a false message

Like Elliot, many young athletes may start using tobacco products in an attempt to reach a certain weight goal.

about weight loss, that influenced his decision to smoke.

Elliot didn't realize that the powerfully addictive quality of nicotine makes smoking extremely habit-forming. Like other smokers, Elliot would have a very difficult time quitting cigarettes. In fact, he may have just begun a lifetime of smoking, possibly a short life-time. His friends wanted to help him lose weight, but did they help him? It's important to recognize when hidden aspects of an activity and incomplete messages about that activity, delivered through direct and indirect peer pressure, are influencing our decisions.

What We Have Learned So Far

The behaviors of others and the media influence our atti-tudes about smoking. We need to be able to recognize when cigarettes and smoking are linked with images designed to "sell" concepts like sophistication, glamour, relaxation, and the "good life."

The decision to start using tobacco products is grounded in social, personality, and attitudinal factors. Therefore, you need to view criti-cally the perspectives, habits, and attitudes reflected by role models and peers, and in the media. By doing this, you'll develop a rea-soned and objective understand-ing of why you are forming par-ticular views about cigarettes. This will guide you as you make personal decisions about smoking.

In this book, you've read about the things that led several people to decide to begin smoking. People start smoking for a variety of reasons, many based on misconceptions and negative peer pressure. The media can influence attitudes about smoking by exposing large audiences to a form of indirect social pressure. When smoking is portrayed as a normal activity, it can give people who smoke, or those who are thinking of trying it, a feeling of belonging. This is falsely reassuring and comforting for those people, and this sense of belonging can certainly influence attitudes about smoking, overriding their better judgment.

In the next chapter, we will learn more about ways that implied messages of social acceptance can influence choices and decisions about smoking. Knowing about these things may help prevent us from drawing false conclusions from the messages and attitudes about smoking we see portrayed in the media.

CHAPTER 4

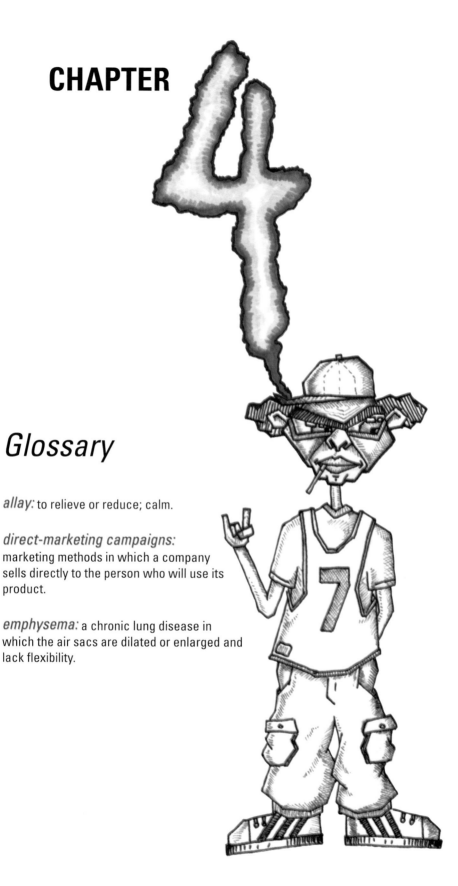

Glossary

allay: to relieve or reduce; calm.

direct-marketing campaigns: marketing methods in which a company sells directly to the person who will use its product.

emphysema: a chronic lung disease in which the air sacs are dilated or enlarged and lack flexibility.

Everyone Smokes: Truth or Lie?

The lights in the theater had dimmed, the movie trailers were over, and it was finally time for the feature to begin. Sultry music played in the background as a small white dot in the center of the screen grew larger to reveal a well-appointed living room in a high-class apartment. A beautiful woman in a soft, fluffy sweater and slim, tailored slacks sat on a white sofa, her legs curled underneath her. As she paged through a magazine, she leaned forward and casually flicked ashes from the tip of her cigarette into a crystal ashtray on the coffee table.

Smoking ads rarely show the most serious health consequences that can result from using their products. However, ads have come a long way since this Chesterfield ad featuring Ronald Reagan!

View Media Critically

Think back to media depictions of smoking you have seen over the years. Smoking is rarely depicted as negative. Its serious health consequences are rarely mentioned, or even hinted at. Evidence of the addictive qualities of nicotine and the resulting habit-forming nature of smoking are also missing from direct and indirect messages presented in cigarette ads. Instead, advertisers use enticing images and familiar scenarios to associate their products with groups of happy, cool, attractive, independent-looking people. This can give the impression that it is "normal"—even desirable—to smoke, and that more people smoke than really do. Contrary to how it might seem through media images, not everyone smokes.

Advertisers attempt to convey the idea that smoking is widespread by using images and settings that depict tobacco use in a wide variety of settings. This can make it appear as if more people smoke than actually do. Teens often overestimate the number of people who smoke. In some studies, teens overestimated the number of peers who smoked by more than five times! Most teens—and others—don't want to feel as though they are the only ones not doing the popular thing. Many are more likely to take that first cigarette if they believe "everyone else" is doing it too. And once

But All My Friends Smoke

It might seem like that, but it's probably not true. According to the 2005 Monitoring the Future Survey, fewer than 25 percent of high school students smoke.

they begin doing something—including smoking—they are inclined to try to get others to do it as well. Young people may be misled into thinking that smoking is no big deal. When they're led to believe that many people smoke, and the messages conveyed by multiple media outlets fail to show the dangerous side effects, viewers (especially young people) may begin to wonder how dangerous smoking really is.

Health Risks of Smoking

Numerous health risks are associated with tobacco use. This activity is so dangerous, that the government

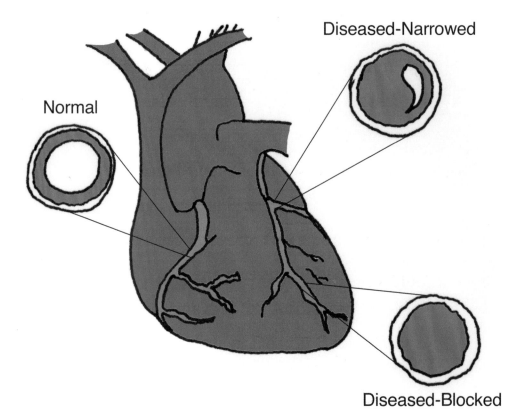

One of the possible life-threatening diseases due to smoking is caused by the narrowing of the arteries due to tobacco smoke. This can lead to an increase in the possibility of strokes or heart attacks.

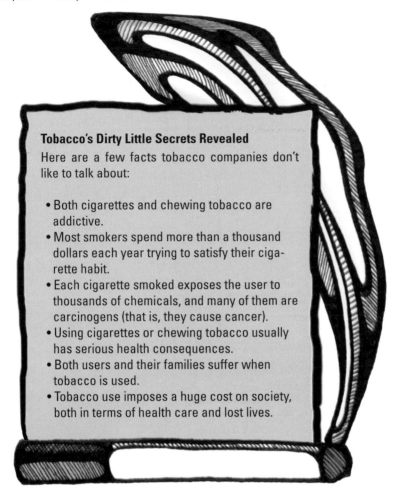

Tobacco's Dirty Little Secrets Revealed

Here are a few facts tobacco companies don't like to talk about:

- Both cigarettes and chewing tobacco are addictive.
- Most smokers spend more than a thousand dollars each year trying to satisfy their cigarette habit.
- Each cigarette smoked exposes the user to thousands of chemicals, and many of them are carcinogens (that is, they cause cancer).
- Using cigarettes or chewing tobacco usually has serious health consequences.
- Both users and their families suffer when tobacco is used.
- Tobacco use imposes a huge cost on society, both in terms of health care and lost lives.

requires warning labels about its health effects to be printed on the side of every package that contains a tobacco product. There is no doubt that smoking is bad for your health; it can even kill you. It can cause diseases of the heart and lungs, such as heart attacks, strokes, hardening of the arteries, blood clots, chronic bronchitis, and *emphysema*.

Most people are aware that smoking triggers lung cancer, the leading cause of cancer death in the United States. But less well known is that cancers of the esophagus, larynx, kidney, pancreas, and cervix are also linked

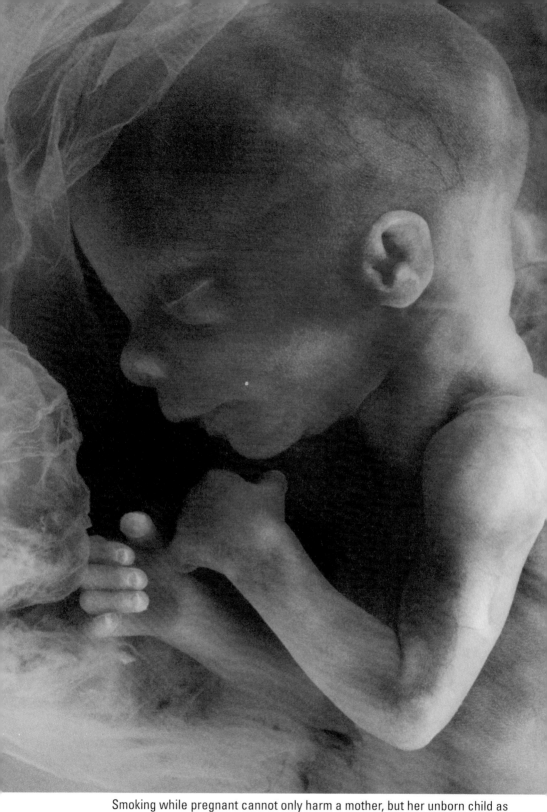

Smoking while pregnant cannot only harm a mother, but her unborn child as well. Smoking can lead to low birth rate and an increase in the chance of premature birth.

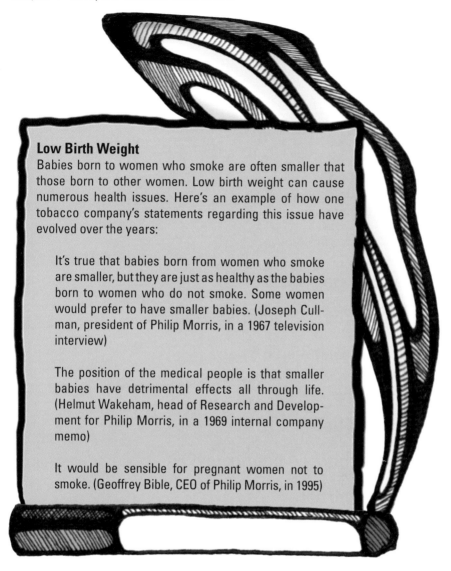

Low Birth Weight

Babies born to women who smoke are often smaller that those born to other women. Low birth weight can cause numerous health issues. Here's an example of how one tobacco company's statements regarding this issue have evolved over the years:

It's true that babies born from women who smoke are smaller, but they are just as healthy as the babies born to women who do not smoke. Some women would prefer to have smaller babies. (Joseph Cullman, president of Philip Morris, in a 1967 television interview)

The position of the medical people is that smaller babies have detrimental effects all through life. (Helmut Wakeham, head of Research and Development for Philip Morris, in a 1969 internal company memo)

It would be sensible for pregnant women not to smoke. (Geoffrey Bible, CEO of Philip Morris, in 1995)

to smoking. Smoking also increases the risk of premature birth and low birth weight in babies whose mothers smoke. Secondhand smoke, or smoke that floats into the air from the end of a burning cigarette, is harmful to the people around anyone who is smoking.

Tobacco ads often portray smoking as glamorous; one company that markets tobacco specifically to women shows the people using their product as beautiful, feminine, and independent.

Advertising

Tobacco companies can no longer use direct advertising on television or radio to sell cigarettes, so they use methods such as sponsorships, product placement, and other less direct means. They may name their cigarettes to evoke a sense of affiliation or familiarity to groups within target markets. For example, ads used by one cigarette maker marketing to women conjured up images of sleekness, femininity, and independence. For many years, another manufacturer used a cartoon camel to project a silly but somehow "cool" image for its cigarettes.

Before the advertising ban, tobacco companies spent a great deal of time, energy, and billions of dollars to create images in ads and commercials of people smoking while engaging in a variety of activities—from fishing, horseback riding, and picnicking, to having fun at parties—in order to link cigarettes to socially desirable role models and situations. Many ads exerted indirect pressure on people to smoke by presenting smokers as glamorous, sophisticated, and independent.

The following historical examples illustrate some strategies cigarette manufacturers used in the past to market their products. Studying these examples might make it easier for you to recognize when you and your peers are the target of indirect peer pressure delivered through a marketing campaign by cigarette manufacturers. Even though tobacco companies can't place ads on television or use *direct-marketing campaigns* that target teens as they used to, the images and subtle techniques from the past still filter into movies and other aspects of popular culture today. When we view marketing critically, we make it difficult for product manufacturers to "pull the wool over our eyes" by using distorted images and references to make their products seem normal, "cool," or otherwise appealing.

Historical Examples

In the early years of the twentieth century, one manufacturer introduced a women's cigarette with the slogan "Mild as May." Ads targeted females by using the image of a woman's hand reaching for a cigarette. The marketing campaign evolved in the mid-1900s to depict fashion-forward women in posh surroundings, whose children touted the brand to their parents. After other brands had established dominance in the market, this particular brand was removed from store shelves.

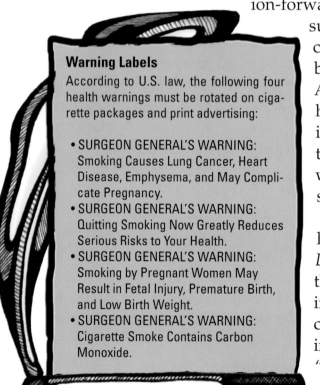

Warning Labels

According to U.S. law, the following four health warnings must be rotated on cigarette packages and print advertising:

- SURGEON GENERAL'S WARNING: Smoking Causes Lung Cancer, Heart Disease, Emphysema, and May Complicate Pregnancy.
- SURGEON GENERAL'S WARNING: Quitting Smoking Now Greatly Reduces Serious Risks to Your Health.
- SURGEON GENERAL'S WARNING: Smoking by Pregnant Women May Result in Fetal Injury, Premature Birth, and Low Birth Weight.
- SURGEON GENERAL'S WARNING: Cigarette Smoke Contains Carbon Monoxide.

In 1952, the popular magazine *Reader's Digest* cast doubt on the wisdom of smoking any brand of cigarette by publishing an article titled "Cancer by the Carton," which linked

LLS'S CIGARETTES.

H. GRAND DUKE NICHOLAS.

WILLS'S CIGARETTES.

FIELD-MARSHAL SIR D. HAIG

Tobacco companies have been using the power of advertising since the beginning of the twentieth century to try to persuade people to choose their brand over others.

smoking to lung cancer and that claimed all cigarettes were lethal. It was later determined that smokers were addicted to nicotine. These events led most smokers to become disenchanted with their old brands or with smoking in general. Advertisers had to come up with new strategies to target customers, who now worried that smoking would lead to lung cancer.

The cigarette producer that had been so successful in the early twentieth century, but whose brand had lost market share by mid-century, reintroduced its product with a completely different image and target market. Its new target consumer was a man who was worried

One cigarette company used a handsome cowboy as a model in an attempt to imply that smoking would make you more attractive and worthy of respect.

about developing lung cancer. The company's ad campaign depicted male role models worthy of respect by other men. Ads featured a smoking cattle rancher and a smoking naval officer. The company added filters to their cigarettes to imply that the product was safer and *allay* cancer fears.

Tobacco Ads Today

In late 1998, the major cigarette manufacturers reached an agreement with forty-six states and

According to U.S. law, the following warning labels must be rotated on packages and advertisements for smokeless tobacco products:

- WARNING: This product may cause mouth cancer.
- WARNING: This product may cause gum disease and tooth loss.
- WARNING: This product is not a safe alternative to cigarettes.

six territories (agreements had already been reached with four other states). Called the Master Settlement Agreement (MSA), the compromise was reached to ward off multitudes of lawsuits against tobacco companies filed by states to recoup some of the money they were forced to spend on medical care for their residents because of tobacco-related health issues. With the settlement, tobacco companies agreed to pay the states more than $240 billion over twenty-five years. The companies also had to agree to change how they marketed their product to limit access to cigarettes by young people. They agreed to bans on:

- the use of cartoon characters in advertising.
- using billboards and other large signs to advertise tobacco products in stadiums and arenas, transit areas like bus shelters and train stations,

video arcades, and shopping malls. (Companies are permitted to place poster-sized ads in some of these areas.)

- tobacco-brand logos on merchandise such as T-shirts, baseball caps, and backpacks, except for certain events sponsored by tobacco companies.
- free product sampling, except for enclosed areas where no minors are present.

- payments for use of cigarettes in movies, television programs, live recorded performances, videos, and video games.
- brand-name sponsorship of concerts, team sports, and events where young people make up a significant portion of the audience, though corporate sponsorship is allowed.

In 1998, cigarette companies met with government officials to reach an agreement called the Master Settlement Agreement, which set rules about how cigarettes and other tobacco products could be marketed.

- sponsorship of events in which minors are contestants or paid participants.

For many years Winston, a cigarette brand, was the primary sponsor of NASCAR racing, one of the most popular sports in the United States. The championship circuit and trophy were called the Winston Cup. Virginia Slims, a cigarette marketed to women, sponsored the women's professional tennis tour. When the MSA limited tobacco companies' sponsorship of major events and their ability to pay for product placement, the companies had to find other ways to promote their products.

According to a study reported in *American Journal of Public Health*, much of tobacco companies' advertising budgets formerly earmarked for billboards has been redirected to point-of-purchase advertising. These are the posters and other ads displayed where cigarettes and other tobacco products are sold. Many critics have complained that these ads are placed at the eye level of young people—even children—rather than adults. Others have complained that there are more ads for tobacco products than there are for healthy items like milk and fruit.

Though tobacco companies can no longer pay to have their products showcased in films, that doesn't mean smoking itself is not featured prominently in movies. Critics have spoken out against the prevalence of smoking in many of the most popular films. This is a trend that may be on the downswing. Several cigarette manufacturers have vowed to discourage the use of their products in movies.

Advertising strategies are often designed to appeal to our need for social approval. Messages embedded in cigarette marketing generally convey false or misleading ideas about smoking as a way to manipulate us into picking up a harmful habit that is very difficult to break. Whenever you see smoking depicted as a "cool" or sophisticated thing to do, and whenever your friends or other peers try to get you to start smoking, look for the hidden and incomplete messages they're sending your way, as well as the direct and indirect peer pressure.

The pressure to smoke or use other tobacco products is all around us. Though tobacco companies have found their access to young people limited, it's still there. It's up to each one of us to develop the skills necessary to resist negative peer pressure and to build the mental and emotional capacities to counter negative influences.

CHAPTER 5

Glossary

attributes: qualities or characteristics of something or someone.

cajoled: persuaded with gentle but persistent argument; coaxed.

cultivating: developing and nurturing.

self-talk: the things we mentally say to ourselves.
social imperatives: obligations or duties.

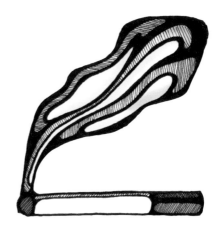

Think on
Your Feet

There's no doubt about it: Resisting peer pressure is not easy. If you're being pressured into smoking, it might help for you to recall the health warnings on cigarette packages, which are listed in chapter 4. Think about the heart and lung diseases smoking causes. Consider, too, that several state governments have sued tobacco companies to recover some of the money they have spent to care for residents who are sick and dying from smoking-related illnesses. Though these lawsuits were settled out of court when tobacco companies agreed to sign the MSA (see chapter 4), these states hold tobacco companies responsible for the illnesses and premature deaths cause by their products. Hopefully, understanding the detrimental health consequences of smoking will be enough to keep you from lighting that first cigarette. If you already smoke, make the life-altering and possibly life-extending decision to quit. You will learn about resources to help you do so in chapter 6.

As you prepare to resist negative peer pressure to smoke or to engage in other unhealthful activities, you may find the strategies outlined here useful. The tips that follow these strategies provide ideas for quick responses in high-pressure situations that can arise from time to time. These tips will help you think on your feet. Being prepared equips you to make the best possible choice when it comes to smoking.

Build Your Self-Esteem

People with healthy self-esteem feel competent and believe they deserve to be happy. Boost your self-esteem by setting reasonable yet challenging goals for yourself and working to achieve them. Treat yourself with compassion, and surround yourself with healthy friends and family members who appreciate and encourage you. Set firm boundaries with people in your life who may not be able to treat you or others respectfully. Healthy self-esteem is an important factor in maintaining resistance to negative peer pressure. Here are some ways to increase your self-esteem:

- Live according to your own core beliefs and values, regardless of what others think. Constantly seeking to impress or gain the approval of others distracts you from living according to your own values. Commit to doing things that reflect your values.

Depression Self-Test

Everyone feels "down" from time to time. If you think you might be more seriously depressed, take this self-test. If you answer yes to even some of these questions, discuss your feelings with your parents and your doctor right away.

- Have you lost interest in hobbies and other activities that used to excite you?
- Do you feel tired most of the time?
- Have your sleeping patterns changed, making it harder for you to sleep or more difficult for you to get out of bed?
- Are you overwhelmed by sadness?
- Do you feel confused or beaten down, as if you cannot stop the pain in your life?
- Are you finding it difficult to go to school and complete assignments or to fulfill your obligations at work?
- Do you feel empty inside?
- Have your eating patterns changed so that you are eating less or more than usual?
- Are you plagued by anxiety or nervousness?
- Do you often feel irritable or restless?
- Are you pessimistic about the future? Does your future look gloomy and difficult to you?
- Would you categorize yourself as pessimistic?
- Are you experiencing digestive problems, headaches, or other physical problems?
- Do you feel lonely and unloved?
- Are *worthless* and *guilt-ridden* terms you would use to describe your feelings?
- Do you feel as if things are out of control and you are helpless to change your situation?
- Does the thought that life is so difficult it is not worth living ever cross your mind?

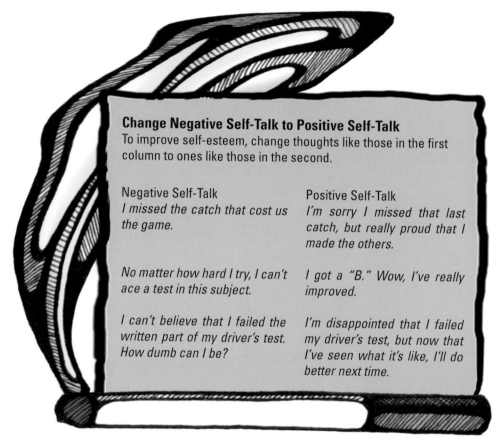

Change Negative Self-Talk to Positive Self-Talk
To improve self-esteem, change thoughts like those in the first column to ones like those in the second.

Negative Self-Talk
I missed the catch that cost us the game.

Positive Self-Talk
I'm sorry I missed that last catch, but really proud that I made the others.

No matter how hard I try, I can't ace a test in this subject.

I got a "B." Wow, I've really improved.

I can't believe that I failed the written part of my driver's test. How dumb can I be?

I'm disappointed that I failed my driver's test, but now that I've seen what it's like, I'll do better next time.

- Set achievable goals and work methodically to accomplish them. This will give you a feeling of self-respect and accomplishment that others cannot provide.
- Counter negative *self-talk* with positive self-talk.
- Take reasonable chances to learn new things and engage in new experiences.
- Face problems and obstacles you encounter by identifying ways to cope with or solve them. Seek the help of trusted advisers when necessary.
- Practice making your own decisions. Realize that your decisions may need to be revised from time

to time, but with practice, you will gain proficiency at making good decisions.

- Acknowledge any limitations you may have, but do not magnify them. Instead, focus on and develop your strengths.
- Accept guidance from others, but rely on your own values and opinions in making choices and decisions.

Build Your Self-Confidence

Self-confident people are self-assured, independent, and secure in their beliefs. They have trust in themselves.

Building self-confidence can make you surer about who you are and what you believe. This can help you resist negative peer pressure.

These *attributes* make them attractive to others. To build your self-confidence, think about what is important to you; identify your own values. Be true to yourself while trying new activities aligned with your own values. Take pride in your accomplishments. Accept responsibility for your actions, and learn how to accept constructive criticism if things sometimes don't work out well. Realize that you are in control of your own life.

Get involved in something outside of your group of friends, for example, by serving as a tutor in your school. This can take the pressure off of you conforming to all of your friends' beliefs and actions.

These actions and attitudes will help increase your self-confidence and your ability to make the choices that are best for you. To read more about increasing self-esteem and self-confidence, check out the books listed in the "Further Reading" section at the back of this book.

Be the Captain of Your Own Ship

Cultivating interests outside those of your peer group is another way to resist negative peer pressure. That's one reason why it's healthy to hang out with people who have different interests than those of your main peer group. Make sure to spend time developing your own interests.

Explore things you like and examine different life directions by getting involved in clubs, sports, hobbies, and other activities. If you're on the track team, try joining the chess club. If you're a good student, offer to tutor others having a hard time. Be honest with yourself about how much pressure you are under to conform to the values and actions of your peer group. Recognizing when you're being pressured to follow a path that doesn't mesh with your values enables you to withstand that pressure and stay true to yourself.

Make Time for Mental Health

Another strategy for resisting negative peer pressure is to take note of your moods and get help if you are depressed. Each of us feels a bit blue or down in the dumps sometimes. This can happen just because you are overtired or have a cold. Most of the time, these periods of sadness are not serious and pass quickly. If you feel down for longer than a week or lose interest in your normal activities and friends, however, you may

Thinking about how to say "no" before you are even offered a cigarette can help you make the right decision when you actually are in that situation.

be more seriously depressed. In a case like this, guard against trying to "tough it out." Instead, get help. Talk to parents, teachers, or trusted friends about how you feel. If you don't know who to ask for help, check with your guidance counselor.

Ace the Academics

Get help with any subjects that are difficult for you. If you have trouble with a particular subject, and fail to address that problem, you might fall into a spiral of lower self-esteem. There is evidence that academic struggles may make people vulnerable to negative peer pressure. Ask a trusted friend, family member, or teacher for advice about how to turn things around. It is important to treat yourself with respect and compassion when you are struggling with a subject. Academic success is a weapon in your arsenal of strategies for resisting negative peer pressure, so be sure to seek out help when you need it.

Just Say No

If you think about ways to say no well before difficult peer-pressure situations arise, you are likely to have a quick, no-nonsense response on the tip of your tongue when you need it. This will help you resist the urge to "go along with the crowd" if you are feeling pressured by your peers to smoke. Here are some ways to say no to tobacco use:

- I don't think so.
- Not interested.
- My coach would kill me.
- Not me, thanks.

- That's okay, I'm good.
- No worries, I don't need it.
- No, thanks.
- I'm outta here.

The strategies and tips in this chapter comprise a sampling of things that can help a person resist negative peer pressure. You can probably think of other ways to say no and to let your peers know that you won't be taunted, *cajoled*, or pressured into smoking or doing anything else you don't want to do. But friends are only one influence. People must also withstand the impact of manipulative advertising.

More Reasons to Avoid Tobacco

There are many reasons not to smoke. If you feel pressured by your friends, and need to quickly recall why you don't want to smoke, call these thoughts to mind:

- Smoking is not attractive. Residue from smoke stains teeth and can make a person's face prematurely wrinkled. It also makes clothes, hair, and breath smell stale and foul. This smell lingers long after the last puff of a cigarette.
- Smoking is detrimental to a person's physical health. It causes respiratory problems, heart disease, and cancer. It diminishes the ability to perform athletically, and can eventually take the smoker's life.

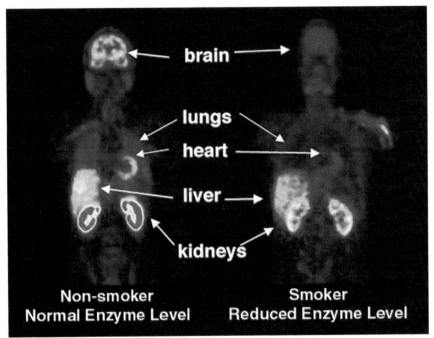

Smoking can reduce enzymes throughout the body, leading to health problems.

- Secondhand smoke is dangerous. It is unappealing, and it harms the health of other people.
- Cigarettes cost a lot of money. People with the habit of smoking a pack each day spend about $1,500 a year trying to satisfy this addiction. Think of other ways this money could be spent.

What We Have Learned

We have learned how to tell when we may be vulnerable to negative peer pressure. Many factors can make us particularly susceptible. We understand that peer pressure can undermine our core beliefs, and that can impact our self-confidence and self-esteem.

We've also learned to view our peers and the media critically in order to avoid developing false impressions about behaviors and habits simply because they are presented as socially acceptable or desirable. Beyond this, we've uncovered strategies used by tobacco companies to link smoking with attractive people and lifestyles. Finally, we have learned tips and ideas intended to fortify our personal character by building or bolstering high self-esteem and healthy self-confidence.

When we are exposed to messages or pressures that involve half-truths presented as *social imperatives*, it is

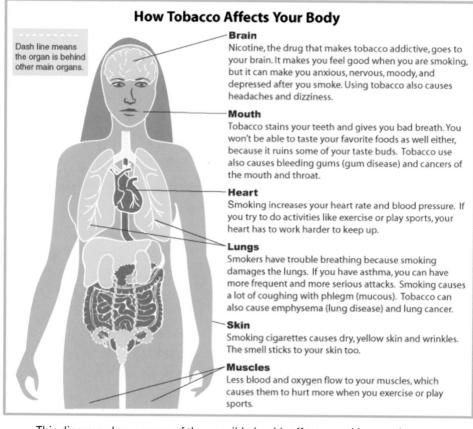

This diagram shows many of the possible health effects smoking can have on the body.

essential to respond negatively in order to maintain our mental and physical health. We recognize the need to be alert to messages designed to create a feeling of inclusion just to capitalize on the very human need to belong, and to react to them appropriately in order to sustain our personal integrity.

If a person has begun to smoke or is having problems standing up to peer pressure to do so, all is not lost. There are organizations available to help.

CHAPTER 6

Glossary

array: a large number or a wide range of things.

covert: not intended to be known, seen, or found out.

onslaught: something resembling a fierce attack.

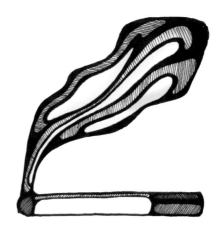

Somebody to Help

Many people succumb to the different forms of peer pressure exerted by those who smoke. Sometimes people try things like cigarettes and regret it later because they get "hooked" before they know it. Quitting can be painful and difficult. If you or someone you know is in this position, many people and organizations stand ready to help.

Nicotine's Hold

Nicotine is a chemical that occurs naturally in the tobacco plant. It is a powerfully addictive substance. Unfortunately, nicotine creates cravings for more nicotine within a very short time. Trying to curb the addiction by stopping smoking can create some very unpleasant symptoms, as noted below. This list of withdrawal symptoms underscores why it is very difficult for many people to quit smoking once they start:

- anxiety
- cigarette cravings
- constipation
- decreased heart rate
- depression
- difficulty concentrating
- fatigue
- headache
- increased appetite
- increased coughing
- insomnia
- irritability or anger
- restlessness
- tremors

Kids Want to Quit Smoking
According to the American Lung Association, when asked, most adolescents who have smoked at least 100 cigarettes in their lifetime report they would like to quit, but are not able to do so.

Ask a Friend for Help

Congratulate yourself for having the guts to admit that you need help to quit smoking and go for it. You might start by asking a trusted friend for help to quit smoking. If you know someone who has quit the habit successfully, ask her for advice. A close friend may also have a parent or other loved one who can give suggestions and tips on how to quit.

Ask Somebody at School

Check with a trusted teacher, counselor, or school nurse to see if your school has a smoking-cessation program.

If your school doesn't, don't worry. You can find help outside of school by contacting other organizations.

Ask a Doctor

A doctor is an obvious choice for help with quitting smoking. Physicians have many tools to help their patients successfully stop smoking. Contact a doctor to discuss nicotine patches and other medicines that can help you quit tobacco.

For many people, medication is the key to getting through the first weeks or months without cigarettes.

Friends can help support you in your attempt to quit smoking.

The U.S. Food and Drug Administration (FDA) has approved seven medications to help smokers quit. Five work to manage withdrawal symptoms and urges by providing small amounts of nicotine. These smoking-cessation medications are available to adults at local pharmacies without a prescription, but minors must have a prescription

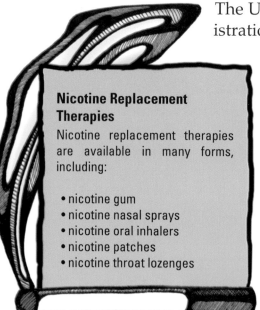

Nicotine Replacement Therapies

Nicotine replacement therapies are available in many forms, including:

- nicotine gum
- nicotine nasal sprays
- nicotine oral inhalers
- nicotine patches
- nicotine throat lozenges

tion from a doctor in order to obtain these nicotine replacement therapies. The other two options are prescription drugs that curb cravings for cigarettes. A doctor can help a person determine what options are best for him and might also recommend counseling to help with the stress of quitting.

Contact Professional Organizations

Many organizations offer programs and other forms of support to help people quit smoking. If you want to stop using tobacco, check out the organizations listed in "For Further Information" at

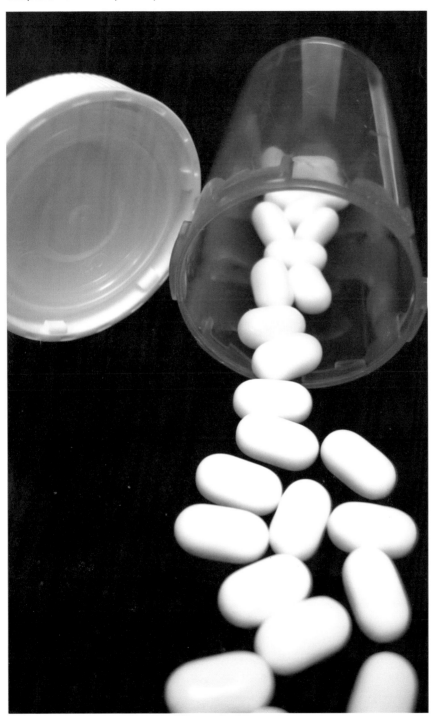

There are many medications that can be used to help stop nicotine cravings. While many of these are available at your local pharmacies, minors may need a prescription from a doctor in order to purchase them.

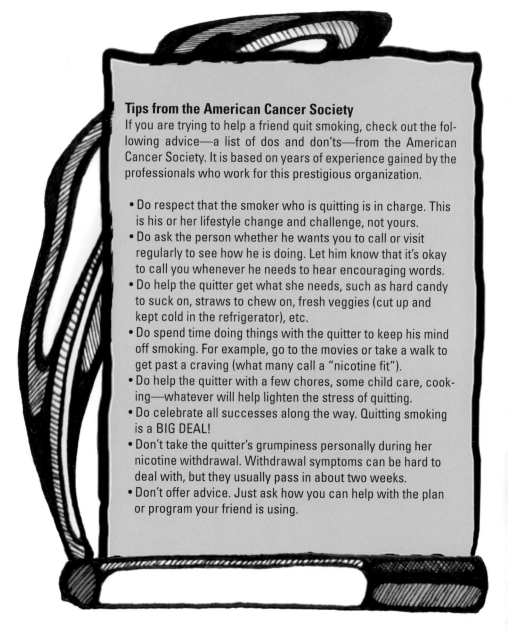

Tips from the American Cancer Society
If you are trying to help a friend quit smoking, check out the following advice—a list of dos and don'ts—from the American Cancer Society. It is based on years of experience gained by the professionals who work for this prestigious organization.

- Do respect that the smoker who is quitting is in charge. This is his or her lifestyle change and challenge, not yours.
- Do ask the person whether he wants you to call or visit regularly to see how he is doing. Let him know that it's okay to call you whenever he needs to hear encouraging words.
- Do help the quitter get what she needs, such as hard candy to suck on, straws to chew on, fresh veggies (cut up and kept cold in the refrigerator), etc.
- Do spend time doing things with the quitter to keep his mind off smoking. For example, go to the movies or take a walk to get past a craving (what many call a "nicotine fit").
- Do help the quitter with a few chores, some child care, cooking—whatever will help lighten the stress of quitting.
- Do celebrate all successes along the way. Quitting smoking is a BIG DEAL!
- Don't take the quitter's grumpiness personally during her nicotine withdrawal. Withdrawal symptoms can be hard to deal with, but they usually pass in about two weeks.
- Don't offer advice. Just ask how you can help with the plan or program your friend is using.

the back of this book. You can also speak with someone who can help by calling the American Cancer Society at 1-800-ACS-2345.

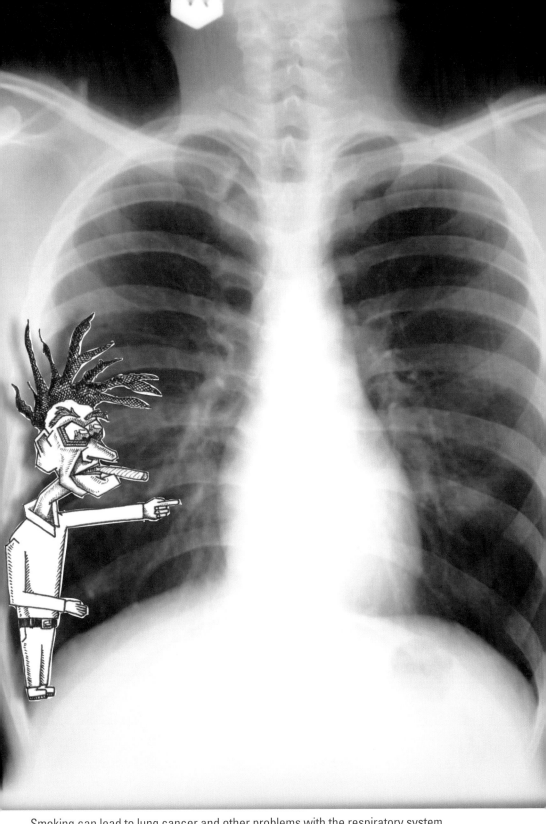

Smoking can lead to lung cancer and other problems with the respiratory system.

What We Have Learned

We've discussed positive and negative peer pressure in this book. We've learned how to recognize when you are being influenced in either a good or a bad way by the actions, habits, and attitudes of others. We discussed why people start smoking in the first place, covering an *array* of factors that influence people to smoke. Knowing these key factors is essential to resisting peer pressure to do something that goes against your values and beliefs. We also talked about how to bolster your self-confidence and self-esteem so you can withstand the *onslaught* of negative influences from others and live your own life.

Now that you know how *covert* messages in television shows, movies, and other media can use misleading references and depictions of lifestyles laden with partial truths to influence people, you are equipped to view these media critically. This will lessen their impact on shaping your values. The glimpse offered in this book into the advertising and marketing strategies employed by tobacco sellers will help you recognize when you are in danger of being

Don't Sabotage a Quitter's Efforts

If you have a friend or loved one who is trying to quit, but you yourself are a smoker:

- If you must smoke, do it outside and always away from the quitter.
- Do keep your cigarettes and matches out of sight. They might be temptations to the person trying to quit.
- Don't ever offer the quitter a smoke, even in jest.
- Do make an effort to quit. It's better for your health and might be easier to accomplish with someone else who is trying to quit.

(Source: American Cancer Society.)

duped by selling techniques and not receiving the complete facts.

Those who are already smokers have gained insight into things that may have caused them to take up the habit. Exposure to tips about how to quit (and about how to assist someone else who wants to quit), and information about where to turn for help, make it possible to select the best option to quit smoking (or help someone else do so). This is a powerful set of resources. They will support and expand efforts to prevent smoking-related diseases and their associated human suffering.

Now it's up to you. Make the decisions that reflect your values in order to live long and to make the most of your life.

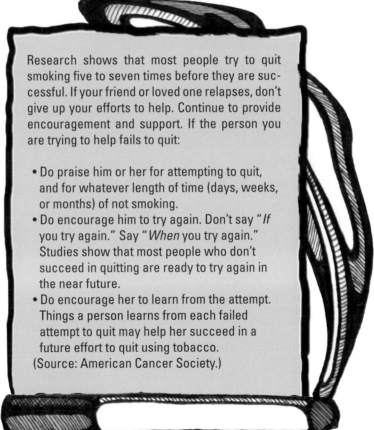

Research shows that most people try to quit smoking five to seven times before they are successful. If your friend or loved one relapses, don't give up your efforts to help. Continue to provide encouragement and support. If the person you are trying to help fails to quit:

- Do praise him or her for attempting to quit, and for whatever length of time (days, weeks, or months) of not smoking.
- Do encourage him to try again. Don't say "*If* you try again." Say "*When* you try again." Studies show that most people who don't succeed in quitting are ready to try again in the near future.
- Do encourage her to learn from the attempt. Things a person learns from each failed attempt to quit may help her succeed in a future effort to quit using tobacco.
(Source: American Cancer Society.)

Further Reading

Desetta, Al (ed.). *The Courage to Be Yourself: True Stories by Teens About Cliques, Conflicts, and Overcoming Peer Pressure*. Minneapolis: Free Spirit, 2005.

Esherick, Joan. *Clearing the Haze: A Teen's Guide to Smoking-Related Health Issues*. Philadelphia: Mason Crest, 2005.

Gately, Iain. Tobacco: *A Cultural History of How an Exotic Plant Seduced Civilization*. New York: Grove Press, 2001.

Heyes, Eileen. Tobacco U.S.A.: *The Industry Behind the Smoke Curtain*. Minneapolis: Twenty-First Century Books, 1999.

Hyde, Margaret O., and John F. Setaro. *Smoking 101: An Overview for Teens*. Minneapolis: Twenty-First Century Books, 2005.

Keyishian, Elizabeth. *Everything You Need to Know about Smoking*. New York: Rosen, 2000.

Stewart, Gail B. *Understanding Issues: Smoking*. San Diego: KidHaven Press, 2002.

For More Information

American Cancer Society's Complete Guide to Quitting
www.cancer.org

American Council on Science and Health
www.theScooponSmoking.org

American Heart Association
americanheart.org

American Lung Association's Freedom from Smoking Online
www.lungusa.org

Center for Tobacco Cessation
www.ctcinfo.org

Centers for Disease Control and Prevention (CDC)
www.cdc.gov/tobacco

CDC's Useful Resources to Quit Smoking
www.cdc.gov/tobacco/how2quit.htm

Medications That Can Help
www.philipmorrisusa.com/en/quitassist/quitting/
medication.asp

National Association for Self-Esteem
www.self-esteem-nase.org/whatisselfesteem.shtml

National Cancer Institute
www.nci.nih.gov

Nicotine Anonymous
www.nicotine-anonymous.org

North American Quitline Consortium
www.naquitline.org

Office of the Surgeon General
www.surgeongeneral.gov/tobacco

QuitNet
www.quitnet.com

Smokefree.gov
www.smokefree.gov/info.html
1-800-QUITNOW (1-800-784-8669)

Publisher's note:
The Web sites listed on this page were active at the time of publication. The publisher is not responsible for Web sites that have changed their addresses or discontinued operation since the date of publication. The publisher will review and update the Web-site list upon each reprint.

Bibliography

American Cancer Society. "Helping a Smoker Quit: Do's and Don'ts: General Hints for Friends and Family." http://www.cancer.org/docroot/PED/content/PED_10_3x_Help_Someone_Quit.asp?sitearea=PED.

American Heart Association. "Smoking and Cardiovascular Disease." http://americanheart.org.

Myrick, R. D., and D. L. Sorenson. *Peer Helping: A Practical Guide.* Minneapolis: Educational Media Corporation, 1988.

SceneSmoking.org. "Dartmouth Study Links Smoking to Smoking in Movies." http://www.scenesmoking.org/news/news10.htm.

University of Rochester. "Advertising Marlboro: Cultural and Historical Perspectives on Cigarette Consumption." http://www.courses.rochester.edu/foster/ANT226/Spring01/history.html.

University of Texas. "Tobacco Cessation Programs Take on Customized Approach." http://www.mdanderson.org/patients_public/prevention/display.cfm?id=2C51024D-37E1-4269-9C526704C6EA6000&method=displayFull&pn=cb7983f9-7868-11d4-aec400508bdcce3a.

University of Texas Student Learning Resources: Strategies for Building Self-Esteem. http://www.utexas.edu/student/utlc/lrnres/handouts/1914.html.

Wakefield, M. A., Y. M. Terry-McElrath, F. J. Chaloupka, D. C. Barker, S. S. Slater, P. I. Clarke, and G. A. Giovino. "Tobacco Industry Marketing at Point of Purchase After the 1998 MSA Billboard Advertising Ban." *American Journal of Public Health* 92 (June 2002): 937–940.

Index

advertising 71–72, 75, 78, 90, 102

American Cancer Society 100, 101, 103

American Heart Association 49

American Journal of Public Health 78

Archives of Pediatrics & Adolescent Medicine 50

behavior 13–15, 24, 27, 45, 47, 60, 92

birth weight 69

Cancer 28, 44, 67, 72, 74–75

lung 67, 72, 74–75

mouth 75

chewing tobacco 21, 28, 67

cigarettes

and peer pressure 13–14, 18, 21–22, 26, 31–32, 51–52, 59

health risks of 17, 18, 28, 44, 49, 60, 66–70, 74, 81, 90–92, 95–100

media portrayal of 46–47, 52, 54, 60–61, 63–65, 78–79

cost of 91

consequences

of peer pressure 15–17, 26, 31–32, 51, 59, 82, 92

of smoking 28, 44, 49, 60, 66–70, 74, 81, 90–92

depression 83

emphysema 62, 67, 72

Food and Drug Administration (FDA) 98

health

risks 17–19, 28, 44, 49, 60, 66–70, 74, 81, 90–92, 95–100

problems associated with smoking 67

heart disease 49, 72, 90

individuality 14

integrity 10, 29, 93

Master Settlement Agreement (MSA) 75–78

media 46–47, 52, 54, 60–61, 65–66, 91, 102

nicotine

addiction 28, 56, 60, 65, 67, 74, 92, 95–100

withdrawal 96, 98

replacement therapies 98

peer pressure

direct peer pressure 21, 26, 31–32, 51, 81–82

indirect peer pressure 21–22, 26, 31–32, 51–52, 59, 71, 81

positive peer pressure
14–15, 26
negative peer pressure 15–17,
26, 31–32, 51, 59, 82, 92
strategies for resisting 35–43,
47, 65, 82–89, 92
pulmonary disease 47, 67

second-hand smoke 28, 69, 90
self-awareness 29, 45
self-confidence 17, 29, 32, 35,
37, 41, 43, 85–87, 91–92, 102
self-esteem 32, 35–37, 82–87
self-talk 84
social interaction 13–14, 17,
21, 27, 29, 35, 42, 44, 47–48,
51–53, 59–61, 71, 79, 92

smoking and peer pressure
13–14, 18, 21–22, 26, 31–32,
51–52, 59

consequences of 28, 44, 49,
60, 66–70, 74, 81, 90–92
media portrayal of 46–47, 52,
54, 60–61, 63–65, 78–79
    quitting 95–103

tobacco
statistics on usage 22, 23, 25,
43, 50, 59, 65
health risks of usage 28, 44,
49, 60, 66–70, 74, 81, 90–92,
95–96
    marketing 52, 54, 56,
    71–79
companies 54, 56, 67, 71,
75–76, 78–79, 81, 92

values 10, 14, 15, 17, 29,
37–38, 42–43, 82, 85–87,
102–103

Picture Credits

Artville: p. 50

Centers for Disease Control
and Prevention: p. 43

Dreamstime
   Redbaron: p. 20

Girlshealth.gov: p. 92

istockphoto.com: pp. 12, 44
   Ball, Jan: p. 32
   Cjmckendry: pp. 95, 97
   Ericsphotography: p. 42
   Monu, Nicolas: p. 45
   Patterson, Anita: p. 34
   Randall Schwanke,
      Randall: p. 99
   Strickke: p. 39
   Tucker, Suzanne: p. 55

National Institute on Drug
Abuse (NIDA), p.91

National Library of
Medicine: p. 77

Jupiter Images: pp. 16, 36,
39, 46, 73, 86, 88

PhotoDisc: p. 57

Office of Applied Statistics:
pp. 25, 59

Stockbyte: p. 71

Tobbaccodocuments.org
   Liggett: p. 64

Author/Consultant Biographies

Author

Lesli B. Evans has spent her entire career in education and educational publishing. She is responsible for creating materials in math, science, health, social studies, and reading for many educational publishing companies. Before starting Professional ED Corporation, she was a liaison with the Florida Department of Education. A graduate of the University of Florida, she was a classroom teacher in Florida before going into educational publishing.

Consultant

Wade Berrettini, the consultant for *Smoking: The Dangerous Addiction*, received his MD from Jefferson Medical College and a PhD in Pharmacology from Thomas Jefferson University. For ten years, Dr. Berrettini served as a Fellow at the National Institutes of Health in Bethesda, Maryland, where he studied the genetics of behavioral disorders. Currently Dr. Berrettini is the Karl E. Rickels Professor of Psychiatry and Director, Center for Neurobiology and Behavior at the University of Pennsylvania in Philadelphia. He is also an attending physician at the Hospital of the University of Pennsylvania.

Dr. Berrettini is the author or co-author of more than 250 scientific articles as well as several books. He has conducted ground-breaking genetic research in nicotine addiction. He is the holder of two patents and the recipient of several awards, including recognition by Best Doctors in America 2003–2004, 2005–2006, and 2007–2008.